*Blackberry Ink*

Berries on the bushes
In the summer sun.
Bring along a bucket
And pluck every one.

Look at my teeth,
They're raspberry red.
Look at my fingers,
They're strawberry pink.
Look at my mouth,
It's huckleberry purple.
Look at my tongue,
It's blackberry ink.

POEMS BY
EVE MERRIAM

*Blackberry Ink*

PICTURES BY HANS WILHELM

A Mulberry Paperback Book / New York

Printed in the United States of America.
First Mulberry Edition, 1994.
10  9  8  7  6  5  4  3  2  1

Library of Congress Cataloging in Publication Data
Merriam, Eve, 1916–  Blackberry ink.
Summary: A collection of humorous and nonsense verses on various themes. 1. Children's poetry, American. [1. Humorous poetry. 2. Nonsense verses. 3. American poetry]  I. Wilhelm, Hans, 1945–  ill.  II. Title.  PS3525.E639B5 1985  811'.54  84-16633
ISBN 0-688-13080-1

To Toby Vera

Bella had a new umbrella,
Didn't want to lose it,
So when she walked out in the rain
She didn't ever use it.

Her nose went sniff,
Her shoes went squish,
Her socks grew soggy,
Her glasses got foggy,
Her pockets filled with water
And a little green froggy.

All she could speak was a weak *kachoo*!
But Bella's umbrella
Stayed nice and new.

I'm a prickly crab,
Know what I can do?
I can scratch, scratch, scratch
Till I scratch on home to you.

I'm a kangaroo,
Know what I can do?
I can jump and thump and bump
Till I jump on home to you.

I'm a wise old owl,
Know what I can do?
I can hoot and hoot and hoot
Till I hoot on home to you.

I'm a downy duck,
Know what I can do?
I can duck down in the water
Till I bob up home to you.

I'm a sandy snail,
Know what I can do?
I can slowly, slowly creep,
till—*z-z-z-z-z*—you're fast asleep.

I'm sweet,
Says the beet.

I'm boss,
Says the sauce.

Oh, no,
Says the dough.

I'm mean,
Says the bean.

Don't be a goop,
Says the soup.

I'll give you a poke,
Says the artichoke.

Go jump in the lake,
Says the chocolate cake.

Please, please,
Says the cheese.

Gooseberry,
Juice berry,
Loose berry jam.

Spread it on crackers,
Spread it on bread,
Try not to spread it
Onto your head.

Gooseberry,
Juice berry,
Loose berry jam.

No matter how neatly
You try to bite in,
It runs like a river
Down to your chin.

Gooseberry,
Juice berry,
Loose berry jam.

Cat's tongue,
Cat's tongue,
Pink as clover.

Cat's tongue,
Cat's tongue,
Wash all over.

Lick your paws,
Lick your face,
The back of your neck
And every place.

Lick your whiskers,
Smooth your fur,
Prick up your ears
And purr, purr, purr.

Cat's tongue,
Cat's tongue,
Pink as clover.

Cat's tongue,
Cat's tongue,
Clean all over.

It fell in the city,
It fell through the night,
And the black rooftops
All turned white.

Red fire hydrants
All turned white.
Blue police cars
All turned white.

Green garbage cans
All turned white.
Gray sidewalks
All turned white.

Yellow NO PARKING signs
All turned white
When it fell in the city
All through the night.

Night-light,
Night-light,
What do you see?
I see you—
Can you see me?

I see a sleepy ceiling,
I see a sleepy floor,
I see soft, sleepy curtains,
I see a sleepy door.

I see a sleepy toy chest,
I see a silent ball,
I see a sleepy picture
Nodding on the wall.

I see a sleepy window,
I see a sleepy chair,
I see a sleepy, sleepy blanket
And a yawning teddy bear.

Night-light,
Night-light,
What do you see?
I see you—
Can you see me?

How do you make a pizza grow?

You pound and you pull and you stretch the dough
And throw in tomatoes and oregano.

Pizza platter for twenty-two,
Pour on the oil and soak it through.

Pizza slices for forty-four,
Chop up onions, make some more.

Pizza pie for sixty-six
With mozzarella cheese that melts and sticks.

Pizza pizza for ninety-nine
With pepperoni sausage ground-up fine.

Pizza pizza stretch the dough,
Pizza pizza make it grow.

"I want my breakfast,"
 The giant said,
"The minute that I wake up
 In my giant bed.

"Tell the kitchen,"
 The giant said,
"I'm giantly hungry,
 And I better get fed.

"I don't want oatmeal
 Or eggs with toast.
 I want what I want
 And I want it the most.

"One hundred pancakes
 And not one less,
 And enough maple syrup
 To make a giant mess."

Caterpillar,
Caterpillar,
Soon
Soon
Soon

Caterpillar,
Caterpillar,
Out
Of your
Cocoon

Fly to Minnesota,
Fly to North Dakota,
Fly to Tallahassee,
Fly to Rome.

Fly to California,
Fly to Philadelphia,
Fly to Appalachia,
Fly to Nome.

Fly to Cincinnati,
Fly to Pensacola,
Fly to Walla Walla,
And then fly home.

Latch, catch,
Come in free.
Catch a ball but you can't catch me.

Latch, catch,
Come in free.
Catch a train but you can't catch me.

Latch, catch,
Come in free.
Catch a fish but you can't catch me.

Latch, catch,
Come in free.
Catch a cold but you can't catch me.

Latch, catch,
Come in free.
Catch your breath but you can't catch me.

Five little monsters
By the light of the moon
Stirring pudding with
A wooden pudding spoon.
The first one says,
"It mustn't be runny."
The second one says,
"That would make it taste funny."
The third one says,
"It mustn't be lumpy."
The fourth one says,
"That would make me grumpy."
The fifth one smiles,
Hums a little tune,
And licks all the drippings
From the wooden pudding spoon.

Xenobia Phobia
Hates to walk,
Xenobia Phobia
Hates to talk.

Xenobia Phobia
Hates to ride,
She hates the city
And the countryside.

Hates her father,
Hates her mother,
Hates her sister
And baby brother.

Hates her uncles,
All her aunts,
Hates her hamster
And the hanging plants.

She hates the circus,
Hates the zoo,
Hates birthday parties
And the color blue.

She hates to dance
And hates to sing.
Xenobia loves
To hate everything.

I have a little dog
And his name is Fetch.

Fetch my slippers,
Fetch my socks,
Fetch my rocker
And my music box.

Fetch my teacup,
Fetch my pot,
Fetch my hot plate
And keep it hot.

Fetch my glasses,
Fetch my book,
I'll turn the pages,
But you can take a look.

Fetch my needle,
Fetch my thread,
Fetch my pajamas
And take me to bed.

*C*rick! Crack!
Wind at my back.

*Snit! Snat!*
Snatched off my hat.

*Whew! Whew!*
It blew and it blew.

Snapped at my ears,
Flapped at my shoes,

And now I've got only
One mitten to lose.

Up in the attic there's a great big trunk
Full of jangling jellified Halloween junk:

There's a rusty hinge with a ghastly creak,
A pair of waterproof boots that leak,

A witch's hat, an old Christmas wreath,
A nest for a bat, a monster's teeth,

Ghostly feathers that float in the air,
A leg from a pirate captain's chair,

A skeleton's hand with a bony clutch,
And something that's much too scary to touch.

Lemonade ran out when the pitcher broke.
Put the greasy pan in the sink to soak.

Climb up the chimney, clear out the smoke.
Ride on a broomstick in a witch's cloak.

Bullfrog in the pond, listen to it croak.
All join hands around the big live oak.

Bertie, Bertie,
Dirty Bertie,
Why don't you take a bath?

I do, says dirty Bertie,
I take one every day,
But I lost the stopper for the tub,
So the water runs away.

Bertie, Bertie,
Dirty Bertie,
Why don't you use the sink?

I can't, says dirty Bertie,
The sink is piled too high
With all the mud pies that I make,
I leave them there to dry.

Something's in my pocket,
What do you think?
It's nothing that goes down
The kitchen sink.

It isn't a penny,
It isn't a nail,
It isn't a cookie
That's nice and stale.

It isn't a whistle,
It isn't a stamp,
It isn't a toad
That's nice and damp.

It isn't an eraser
Or a ticket stub,
It isn't a piece
Of pocket flub.

It isn't a ring
Or string
Or a stone,
It isn't a bead
Or a weed
Or a bone.
I won't give it to you—
Get a hole of your own.

Swish, swash,
Washing machine.
Swish, swash,
Make it clean.

Swish, swash,
Bubble and spin.
Swish, swash,
Pack it all in.

Mishmash,
Jeans and sheets,
T-shirts and towels,
And a skirt with pleats.

Mishmash,
Three odd socks,
An old rag doll,
And a terry-cloth fox.

Swish, swash,
Washing machine.
Swish, swash,
Clean all clean.

Is it robin o'clock?
Is it five after wing?
Is it quarter to leaf?
Is it nearly time for spring?

Is it grass to eleven?
Is it flower to eight?
Is it half-past snowflake?
Do we still have to wait?

Left foot,
Right foot,
Where are my slippers?

Left foot,
Right foot,
Where are my sneakers?

Left foot,
Right foot,
Where are my rain boots?

Left foot,
Right foot,
Where are my toes?

They're just where you left them—
On the end of your nose.

Cat cat cat on the bed,
Bed's too soft, it jumps on my head.
Head head, head's too hard,
Cat wriggles out into the yard.
Yard yard, cat slips away
Over to the playground where the children play.
Playground seesaw, who wants to ride?
Cat's all ready on the other side.